# The Wide~Awake Princess

# The Wide~Awake Princess

by KATHERINE PATERSON

illustrated by VLADIMIR VAGIN

CLARION BOOKS ~ NEW YORK

Clarion Books
a Houghton Mifflin Company imprint
215 Park Avenue South, New York, NY 10003
Text copyright © 2000 by Minna Murra, Inc.
Illustrations copyright © 2000 by Vladimir Vagin

The type for this book was set in 14-point Berkeley.
The illustrations were executed in pencil with watercolor.

Printed in Hong Kong.

Library of Congress Cataloging-in-Publication Data

Paterson, Katherine.
The wide-awake princess / by Katherine Paterson ; illustrated by Vladimir Vagin.
p.   cm.
Summary: After the death of her self-absorbed parents, a clever princess
shows the peasants in her country how to make better lives for themselves.
ISBN 0-395-53777-0
[1. Kings, queens, rulers, etc. Fiction. 2. Princesses. Fiction.]
I. Vagin, Vladimir Vasil′evich, 1937–  ill. II. Title.
PZ7.P273Wi    2000
[Fic]—dc21    99-30879
CIP
SCP   10  9  8  7  6  5  4  3  2  1

This book is for Kate Green,
who is wide awake, with love.
—K. P.

To my goodhearted friends,
Nina and Alexander.
—V. V.

Once upon a time, long ago, there lived a king and a queen. They were as rich as royalty should be, but they lacked one thing. Though they had been married many years, they had no heir. When at last a baby princess was born, the whole kingdom rejoiced. I say the whole kingdom rejoiced, but if you looked very carefully, you would have realized that this was not so.

The poor people of the country went to work as usual, and when they got home at night, they were too tired for rejoicing. After a hard day in the fields, most of them fell asleep the minute they laid their heads on their straw mattresses. The rich people found rejoicing a bore, so after a few hurrahs and a toast or two, they went back to their usual selfish and lazy lives. Soon, hardly anyone remembered that the country had a new princess.

The king and queen were a bit annoyed that so little fuss had been made over the royal birth. So their majesties decided to have an enormous celebration and invite all the important people of their little land to a day of feasting and merriment, when they could admire the baby and, naturally, bring her many rich gifts. The appointed day came, and all the food was ready. The footmen stood at the great doors, ready to open them at the first knock, but the knocker was silent.

The king began to be impatient. He opened the great doors himself and peeked out. There was no one to be seen. Where were all the important guests? Where, indeed, were all the rich gifts?

The queen began to cry. Her poor baby. Was there no one who would rejoice at her birth? Were there to be no grand presents to grace the royal nursery?

The household began to grow weary with waiting.

Before long the king and queen fell asleep on their thrones.

Several of the butlers and maids went to sleep on their feet.

The cooks were snoring in the kitchen.

Even the cats and mice and pigs and goats and hounds and horses closed their eyes.

There was no one in the whole castle awake to hear the gentle knock on the great front doors. Nor the second knock. Nor the third. Finally, the doors were shoved open a crack, and a tiny, bent form stuck her head into the hall. She could barely see inside, for the candles had long ago sputtered and died.

"Halloo!" she called out. "Is anyone here?"

There was no answer except a chorus of snores. The little old woman wandered from room to room, looking for someone to whom she might speak, but everyone she saw was fast asleep.

Then from far away in the depths of the castle, she heard a tiny cry. The closer she got to the cry, the louder it became. Finally, she reached the nursery and found the infant princess crying in the royal bassinet—the only creature in the entire castle who was not fast asleep.

The little old woman pulled over a stool and climbed up on it so she could reach the top of the bassinet. She looked down at the red-faced baby. "Hello, there," she said. "Sorry I was late to the party. I started off in plenty of time, but I kept meeting people on the road with spells needing unspelling and curses needing uncursing. So here I am at last. As your fairy god-mother, I was supposed to have brought you a present, but you already have so much. What on earth do you need?"

The little old lady stopped and thought for a moment. "I know!" she said. "I'll give you the gift of being wide awake all your waking hours. With that gift, you can enjoy all your other gifts. Without it, none of the rest matters."

The old woman touched her wrinkled lips with the tip of a crooked finger and then reached down and lightly touched each of the baby's eyelids.

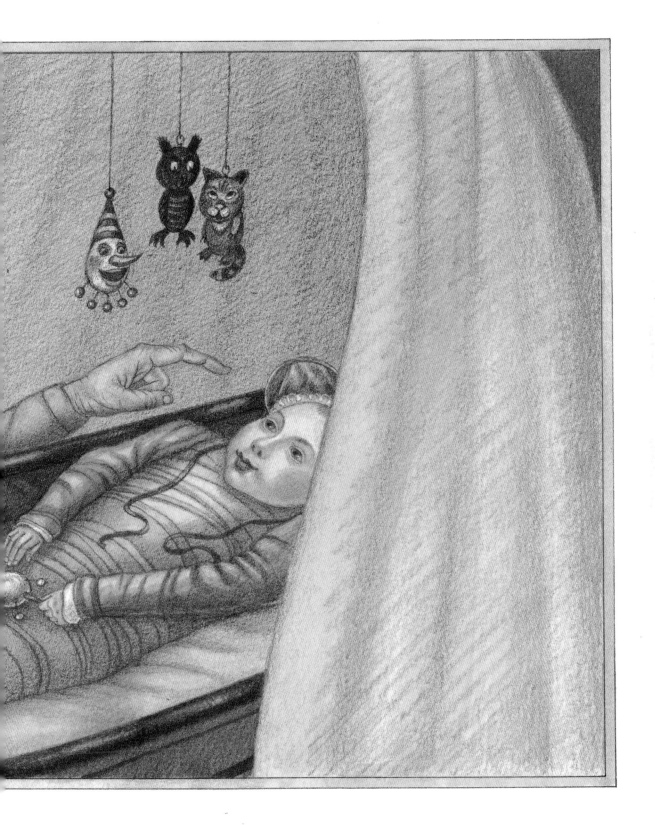

"Wake well, my beauty," she whispered, and, with that, she
was gone.

Princess Miranda didn't remember her god-mother's visit the night of the party, but she grew up different from other princesses. While they were busy trying on fancy dresses and looking into mirrors, Miranda was lying on her stomach, watching an ant crawl across the courtyard carrying a cake crumb three times its size to its hill in the garden.

"Do stop daydreaming!" her governess said through a large yawn, but Miranda wasn't dreaming. She was wide awake with wonder.

She rarely saw the king and queen, who spent their waking hours with the nobility, playing cards, eating and drinking too much, and quarreling and gossiping far too much.

Her governess spent most of her time taking naps, so
Miranda wandered about the castle grounds getting acquainted
with the horses and hounds and goats and chickens.

The year that Miranda was twelve, both her parents died. It was a sad time for Miranda. Her parents had always been so occupied with other people that she felt they had left her before she'd ever really had a chance to know them. She told her sorrows to the animals, her only true friends. One of the young goats and an old hound seemed to understand, and they sat close to her and let her hug them and shed her tears on their warm backs.

One morning she woke up and realized that however sad she felt, there was work to be done. She was queen now, whether she wanted to be or not.

She went down to the throne room. There she found three angry nobles fighting over who should be king.

"What about me?" she asked. "Am I not the queen?"

The nobles turned and looked at her in astonishment. "We've heard about you," the tallest of them said, looking down his long nose. "You're far too short to be queen."

"Don't you know," the oldest one said, "that you are far too young to rule?"

"Besides," said the chubby one, "how can you be queen? You don't even know how to dress properly."

"I could learn how to be queen," Miranda said.

"It's not something you *learn,*" said the tall noble. "It's something you're *born* knowing."

"Oh," said Miranda, and she went back to her room. Her governess was napping as usual, so Miranda decided to go out and take a close look at the kingdom that the nobles thought she was not fit to rule. When the old hound and the young goat saw her saddle her horse, they ran to her side, eager to come along.

Soon the little party came to a sparkling brook spanned by a wooden bridge. Miranda had never crossed that bridge before, but it seemed a good day for an adventure.

"Who's that trespassing on my bridge?" a terrible voice cried out.

"It's only me, Miranda," she answered. "And my friends."

An ugly troll popped out from beneath the bridge. "There's a toll for crossing this bridge," the troll said.

"I'm sorry," Miranda said. "I didn't know that. I don't have any money."

"It's not money I want," said the troll. He gazed up hungrily at the fat little goat. "I'll take that succulent little kid for my supper."

"Oh, I couldn't let you have the goat," Miranda cried. "She is my friend and companion on the road."

"Very well," said the troll. "Just give me that skinny old hound, then. He won't live much longer anyhow."

Miranda was horrified. "What a terrible thing to say," she said. "The hound is my protector, and if you aren't careful, he may decide to take a nip out of you!"

"Oh, very well," the troll said hastily. "The horse will have to do." He came scrambling up the bank and onto the bridge.

Miranda held the horse's reins out of reach. "This is a small horse, but she's three times your size," she said. "You couldn't possibly eat her. Besides, we're going adventuring, and we can't do that without a horse."

Miranda peered down into the troll's ugly face. "You don't look nearly so ferocious as you sound. Are you really a troll?"

The troll began to laugh, and as he did so, he began to change until Miranda saw standing in front of her a little old woman, her face as merry as a summer morning.

"No, I'm not a troll," the old woman said. "I'm your fairy godmother, but I needed to put you to the test. You are not only lovely to look at, you are intelligent and compassionate as well. Now that I know this, you may, if you like, choose to have removed the curse I put upon you the day of your celebration."

"What curse was that?" Miranda asked.

"Why, the curse of being awake all your waking hours."

"Is that a curse?" Miranda was puzzled. Why should she mind being awake from the time she got up in the morning until she went to bed at night? There was so much to do, so much to learn, so much to enjoy in the world. "I like being awake," she said.

"Ah, my child," the old woman said. "If you know that being wide awake in a sleeping world is a gift and not a curse, you are even wiser than I had hoped." The fairy smiled. "Go, then, with my blessing," she said.

"Before I go, may I ask you a question? Is it true that I cannot learn how to be queen?"

The old woman snorted. "Has some fool told you that?"

"The nobles said I must be *born* knowing."

"And what do you think?"

"I think I could learn if I set my mind to it."

"Then what are you waiting for? You must hurry, my child, before those stupid men destroy this kingdom with their lazy, greedy ways."

Miranda decided that a princess learning to be a queen should first get to know the people whom she wished to rule. But if she went around on a horse from the castle, everyone would know who she was before she had a chance to learn anything from them. Sadly, she sent the horse, the hound, and the goat home and began to walk about the land.

All that day and each day after that, she went from field to field and farm to farm and cottage to cottage. She told no one who she was, but simply said that she needed to work for her bread. At first the peasants were suspicious of her, as not many strangers came through the land. But she was cheerful and soon proved to be a hard worker.

The women were happy to let her weed their tiny patches of vegetables or churn their butter or knead their dough. The men were a little slower to accept help from a mere slip of a girl, but there were never enough willing hands and backs, so soon she was cutting hay and binding sheaves and beating the grain from the chaff.

Her hands became rough and her face burned dark by the sun, but she felt sure no one at the castle would notice. No one even seemed to realize that she was gone from sunup to past sundown every day except Sunday the whole summer long.

fter a few weeks, the peasants forgot she was a stranger. They spoke quite openly around her, complaining of their hard lives and the high taxes they were forced to pay.

Miranda listened carefully. She rarely spoke, because she had learned that when you listen you learn a great deal more than when you speak. But when an old man they called Amonth told her of his sick grandchild, who needed fruit and

healing herbs and the care of a physician—all things he could not possibly afford to give her—Miranda could hold her peace no longer. "It's not fair!" she cried out. "Why don't you people revolt?"

Most of the peasants looked at her and laughed bitterly. The old man smiled sadly, and at the end of the day he invited her home to his cottage to meet his family.

Miranda realized that it was a sacrifice for Amonth's family to share its coarse black bread and goat cheese with her, but she was truly hungry. She gratefully ate the portion of food they offered her. She liked being with Amonth's family. He had a widowed daughter, Gwen, and two grandchildren, little Serina, the sick child, and her older brother, Wick, whom Miranda had seen earlier working in the field.

"It is too late for you to be going out alone tonight," Gwen said. "Wick will bring hay from the shed and make up a bed for you with us tonight, if you like." Miranda thanked her, for she was tired and was dreading the long walk back in the dark. No one seemed eager to go to sleep. Gwen went to a loom in the corner of the tiny cottage and began to weave by the light from the dying fire. Amonth took out a wooden flute and began to play, while Wick, to Miranda's great surprise, took a book from a chest and, sitting close to the single candle, began to read.

"Where did you learn to read?" she asked.

"I learned from an old peddler who came here from time to time," the boy answered. "In my foolishness I told him I wanted to be rich, and he gave me this book." He smiled at Miranda through the candlelight. "And now I am."

Miranda wanted to stay awake and watch and listen, but the lilting melody of the flute lulled her to sleep.

Early the next morning, Miranda looked at the tapestry on the loom. Though a large part of it was rolled up out of sight, she saw that the section Gwen was weaving showed a picture of peasants working in the field. "I can't finish it without more thread," Gwen said.

"It's quite beautiful," said Miranda.

"It's the history of our country," said Gwen. "Now that times are so hard and sad, I wanted to remember it was not always this way."

"How was it before?" Miranda asked.

"When I was a little girl, we had a very gracious king who made sure all the people had enough to eat and a good life. After his death, his son . . ." She sighed.

Amonth took up the painful story. "Our recent king never noticed what was going on. He let the greedy nobles raise taxes so high that many of us are suffering from lack of food and clothing." He glanced toward the pale child on the straw mattress near the fire. "Now that he is dead and the nobles are in charge, things are bound to get even worse." He shook his head. "There is nothing we can do."

"You could revolt," said Miranda.

Amonth smiled patiently. "With no arms? With only enough strength to drag to the fields and do our work? No," he said sadly. "We are helpless and ignorant. How could we possibly revolt?"

Instead of going on to another village that day, Miranda went home to the castle. She had to think. If she was going to be queen, she had to figure out how to help her people. There was no one to talk to, so she went out to the barnyard and called her goat and hound, and the three of them went to the stable. There she whispered the problem to her friends.

Miranda told them what she had seen and heard as she had gone around the countryside working with the peasants. She

knew the peasants were not ignorant, but what could she do? She was only a girl—one no one paid attention to. She would somehow have to persuade the people to do what must be done. The animals nodded solemnly. "Then that's it," Miranda said. "They must do it themselves."

The next day she went back to Amonth's cottage. She
brought with her strong broth that the castle cook had made and
some healing herbs. "These are for Serina," she said to Gwen.
Amonth's daughter looked puzzled. She started to ask a question, but she wanted her daughter to get better more than she
wanted to know where Miranda had gotten such expensive
herbs and such rich broth.

While Gwen was heating the broth, Miranda began to tell

the woman what she had been thinking. "There is so much wisdom in this cottage," she said. "If you were to share it, we could help the people see that they do not have to keep on living in misery. In your weaving you have the history of our country. I will bring you thread so that you can finish it. Then you must show it to all the people, so they will know that things have not always been grim. Wick can teach everyone who wishes to learn how to read and write, just as the old peddler taught him, so the people can begin to feel strong and wise and full of hope. And Amonth can help each family to make a musical instrument, because, as you must know, nothing lifts the heart like music."

"You are a very wise child," Gwen said. "Where did you come from and why do you want to help us?"

"My name is Miranda," Miranda said.

"Then you are the lost princess!"

"Is that what they say about me?"

"That is what the nobles said when your parents died and someone asked why you would not be queen." Gwen smiled. "Wick suspected you might come from the castle, but the rest of us looked at your clothes . . . Well, they are a clever disguise."

Miranda looked down at her plain dress. It was the only one she ever wore.

"But why did you leave the castle?" Gwen asked. "Why aren't you queen?"

Miranda sighed. "No one wants a queen who keeps her eyes open," she said. "Please don't tell anyone who I am."

Gwen solemnly agreed to keep Miranda's secret.

Over the next five years things began slowly to change. Serina grew strong and healthy. Then she and her mother went wandering from village to village, showing Gwen's tapestry and telling people the true story of their country. Wherever people listened and asked how they might change things, Wick came to teach them to read. Miranda helped by bringing all sorts of dusty books from the castle library.

Then Amonth played his lovely music. If people said wistfully that they wished they could make such beauty, he would help them carve their own flutes and lyres and fiddles and teach them how to play.

A great difference came over the country. Not magically in a moment, but like yeast working in dough, the spirits of the people began to rise. They worked just as hard every day, and taxes rose every year, but the people were growing stronger and stronger, until one day they said to Amonth, "We've had our fill of tyranny! What must we do?"

On that day Amonth sent Wick to the castle to tell Miranda that the people were ready. She was anxious about what might happen next, but she was determined to do her part.

Meanwhile, Amonth organized nearly a thousand peasants into a great band. They began to march toward the castle. Those who had flutes and lyres and fiddles were in front. The others, who had pots to clash and hollow sticks to beat together, followed behind. Last of all came the blacksmith, with his huge anvil on a cart. Two boys pulled the cart while he clanged down on it with his enormous hammer. The noise shook the road on which they walked.

As soon as Miranda heard the sounds of the band, she rushed to the throne room. "Help! Help!" she cried. "Something terrible is happening!"

The nobles, who had been fighting almost continuously since the last king died, looked up, annoyed to have their quarrel interrupted. In that one moment of quiet, they too heard the strange music coming up the road. They rushed to the windows.

They couldn't see a thousand ragged peasants with homemade instruments. All they could see was a great cloud of dust—the same kind of dust raised by an army of horsemen bent on attack.

"There are so many of them," Miranda cried out. "Surely they will overrun the castle! They will kill us all!"

The tallest noble glanced at the others. "Perhaps not," he said. "Sometimes the enemy is satisfied if the ruler goes out alone and surrenders."

"Oh, yes," said Miranda. "I've read about that. But then they kill the king, and *their* king takes the throne." She looked at the three nobles. "Which of you is king today?"

"Not me!"

"Not me!"

"Not me!"

Suddenly, all three turned and fell like sacks of grain at Miranda's feet. The tall one lifted his head an inch. "The king is dead," he shouted. "Long live the queen!"

"Long live the queen!" echoed the others and dropped their noses to the floor.

"Oh, very well," Miranda said. "If you insist."

Miranda put on queenly robes, called the hound and the goat, and saddled her horse. The band was advancing on the castle. In the lead was a tall white-haired man playing a flute, and beside him a bent little form that, in the dusty light, resembled a troll.

Miranda, wide awake and smiling, rode forth to meet her people.